W9-DDA-827

WITHDRAWN

Learn to Draw Manga

MANGA ANIMALS

Illustrated by
Richard Jones & Jorge Santillan

PowerKiDS
press™

New York

Published in 2013 by The Rosen Publishing Group, Inc.
29 East 21st Street, New York, NY 10010

First Edition

Produced for Rosen by Calcium Creative Ltd
Editor: Sarah Eason
Editor for Rosen: Sara Antill
Book Design: Paul Myerscough

Illustrations by Richard Jones and Jorge Santillan

Library of Congress Cataloging-in-Publication Data

Jones, Richard.
 Manga animals / by Richard Jones & Jorge Santillan. — 1st ed.
   p. cm. — (Learn to draw manga)
 Includes index.
 ISBN 978-1-4488-7872-7 (library binding) —
ISBN 978-1-4488-7943-4 (pbk.) — ISBN 978-1-4488-7949-6 (6-pack)
1. Animals in art—Juvenile literature. 2. Comic books, strips, etc.—
Japan—Technique—Juvenile literature. 3. Cartooning—Technique—
Juvenile literature. I. Santillan, Jorge. II. Title.
 NC1764.8.A54J36 2013
 741.5'1—dc23
                                    2011052876

Manufactured in the United States of America

CPSIA Compliance Information: Batch #B4S12PK: For Further Information contact Rosen Publishing, New York, New York at 1-800-237-9932

Contents

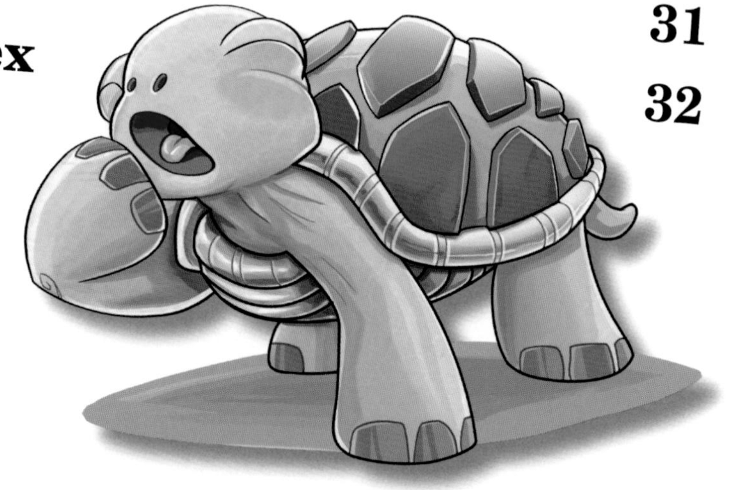

Drawing Manga Animals

"Manga" is a Japanese word that means "comic." Manga animals can be powerful and scary or cute and adorable. Discover how you can draw incredible Manga animals yourself!

Manga animal world

In this book, we are going to show you how to draw some of the most interesting animals in the world, Manga-style!

You will need

To create your Manga animals, you will need some equipment:

Sketchpad or paper
Try to use good quality paper from an art store.

Pencils
A set of good drawing pencils are key to creating great animal drawings.

Eraser
Use this to remove any unwanted lines.

Paintbrush, paints, and pens
The final stage for all your drawings will be to add color. We have used paints to complete the Manga animals in this book. If you prefer, you could use pens.

Colorful Bird

This bright, colorful bird has been styled with a cute Manga look.

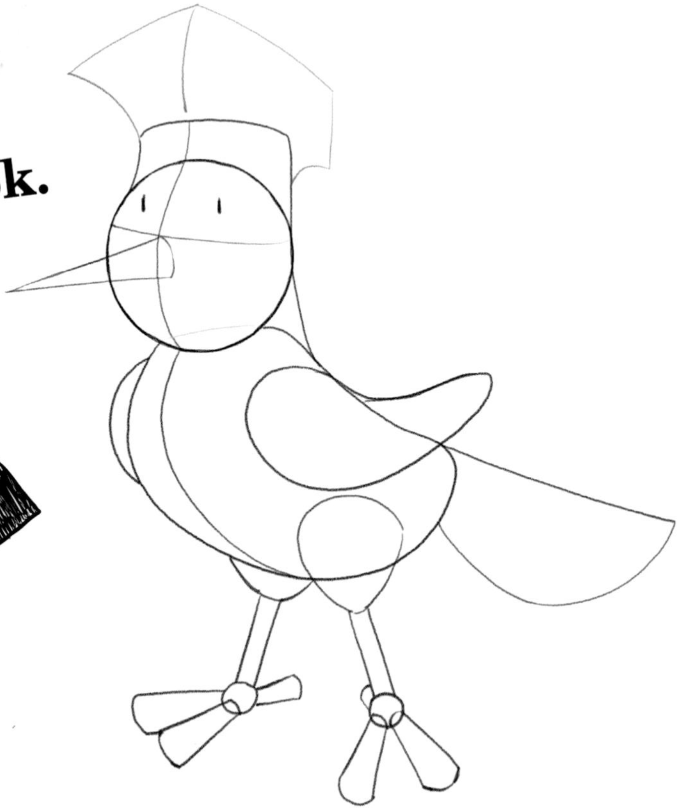

Step 1

Use simple shapes to create the bird's basic outline.

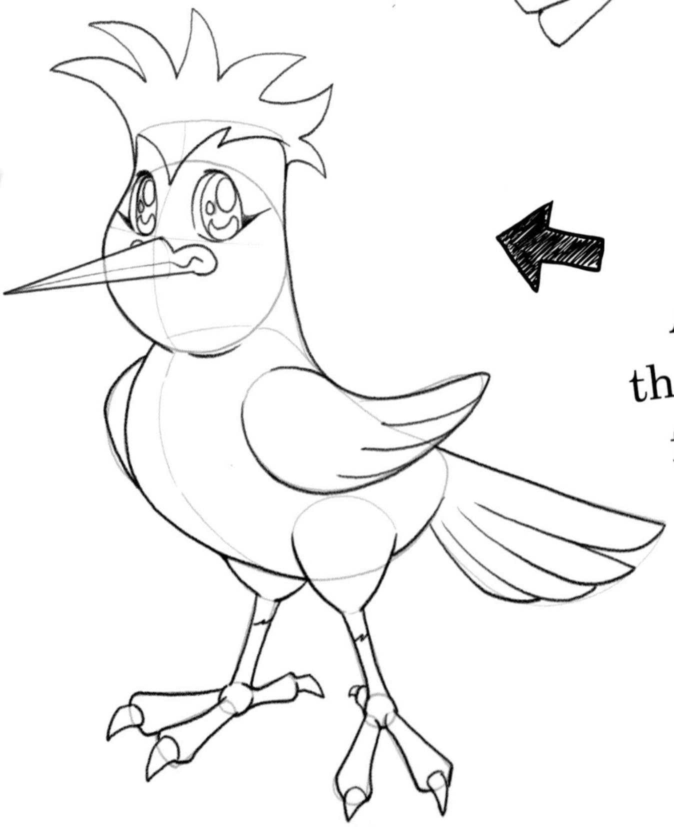

Step 2

Add detailed lines for the head, tail, and wing feathers. Pencil in the eyes and claws.

Step 3

Spend time shading the bird's eyes. They are one of its most important features. Add some more detail to the chest and the wing feathers.

Step 4

Now you can give your bird its beautiful, bright colors. Choose a yellow for the body and a red for the head feathers. Give your bird bright blue eyes. Choose orange for the feet and beak. Add highlights to the head and chest.

Spitting Cobra

This deadly snake raises itself high into the air then lunges forward to bite its victim. Despite its name, it does not spit its venom. Instead, it injects the poison through its fangs.

Step 1

You can create the body and tail for your snake with lots of tube shapes. Add the winglike shapes at the sides of the cobra's head, called the "hood."

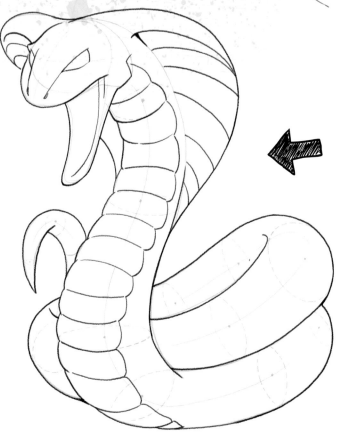

Step 2

Now add lots of lines to the front of the cobra's body and to the hood. Pencil the eyes.

Step 3

Cobras are covered in diamond-shaped scales. Cover the back tail in this pattern. Pencil the fangs and tongue.

Step 4

Go over the diamond-shaped scale pattern with a heavier pencil line. The marks should show through the paint when you color the snake.

Sharpen your skills

Here is another pose to try out.

Step 5

This cobra has a golden body and purple and gold scales. Complete the snake with bright green eyes and a pink tongue. Add a wash of blue beneath the cobra.

River Turtle

Manga animal characters can be really cute and lovable, like this yawning turtle.

Step 1

Draw a large circle for the turtle's body and a smaller circle for the head. Pencil the legs and tail.

Step 2

Go over your outline with a heavier black line. Pencil the eye and shell shapes.

Step 3

Add detail to the eyes. Pencil nostrils and the yawning mouth. Add the shell pattern and the nails on the feet.

Step 4

Your turtle should be a mix of different green and orange colors. Choose a light green for the head and legs. Paint the pattern on the shell a dark green. Use orange for the rest of the shell and add some to the cheeks. Add a wash of blue for the water beneath your animal friend.

Snarling Tiger

The tiger is one of the most awe-inspiring beasts on Earth. We've created this Manga tiger with a wild mane and wild colors!

Step 1

Your tiger should be crouching low, ready to pounce! Draw circles for the body and head outlines. Use ovals for the thighs and shoulders. Pencil the legs, paws, and tail.

Step 2

Add the powerful muscle lines on the shoulders and the opening of the snarling mouth. Add the ears.

Step 3

Draw the huge mane on the tiger's neck and the bushy tail. Add the massive claws, teeth, and fangs. Pencil the eyes.

Step 4

Add the zebralike pattern to the tiger's body, legs, and tail.

Sharpen your skills

You could try a different color palette or another pose.

Step 5

Now bring your tiger to life! To copy this color palette, choose a light blue-gray color for the body, face, and legs. Pick a dark gray for the pattern, bush of the tail, and the ears and mane. Yellow eyes and white fangs and claws complete the tiger.

Hungry Panda

Pandas munch their way through 41 pounds (18.6 kg) of bamboo every day! That's one hungry panda!

Step 1

Give your panda a round head. Choose oval shapes for the arms and feet. Draw a triangle for the body.

Step 2

Mark out the eyes, nose, and mouth. Roughly pencil the ears, claws, and hair.

Step 3

Now add the eyes and the large rings around them. Pencil the teeth, paw marks, and the bamboo.

Step 4

Color the panda's sides, arms, legs, paws, ears, and tail black. Fill in the rings around the eyes. Leave the rest of the panda white. Add a wash of green beneath the panda.

Hunting Dog

This powerful dog is a hunter with powerful legs, a strong body, and jaws that can deliver a killer bite.

Step 1

Your Manga dog is on a chase. Create the running pose with a long, rounded body shape. Pencil the legs, head, ears, and tail.

Step 2

Pencil detail for the eyes, nose, and mouth. Then erase most of the rough inner lines.

Step 3

Add muscle lines to the head and body. Draw the collar and shade the mouth. Pencil the dog's sharp teeth.

Step 4

Use a fine-tipped pencil to add more light shading to the lines of the body.

Sharpen your skills

Dogs are agile animals. Try some different poses.

Step 5

A palette of brown shades is perfect for this hunting dog. Choose a creamy brown for the underbelly. Add light brown to the legs, cheeks, and central part of the face. Use a dark brown for the ears, back, nose, and tail. Paint a red collar with gray studs. Add a wash of blue below the dog.

Wild Horse

Horses are some of the most beautiful and best-loved animals on Earth. Horses like this stallion still run wild in some parts of the world.

Step 1

Your stallion should be rearing up onto its back legs. Use circles to create the head, nose, and body. Use cone shapes for the legs and a crescent shape for the tail.

Step 2

Mark out the eye, lips, ear, and nose. Trace a thicker black line along the outer line of the horse.

Step 3

Add the mane and tail on the horse's neck and head. The mane should be wild and thick. Pencil in the teeth.

Step 4

Add detail to the mane, tail, and legs. Pencil the detail of the eye, nostrils, and teeth.

Sharpen your skills

You can choose any color palette or pattern you like. Try some of these ideas.

Step 5

This Manga horse has a brilliant purple mane and tail. Choose a pale purple for the back, shoulders, and rear. Add light gray to the face, neck, and chest. Use a very pale gray for the spotted pattern. Color the lips and nose black. Use the same color for the legs and hooves. Use white for highlights.

More Animals

If you've loved drawing Manga animals, try some more!

Shark

Try this sleek, fast ocean predator.

Panther

With its daggerlike teeth and sharp claws, the panther is an awesome hunter.

Lizard

This reptile has a frilled neck to scare off predators.

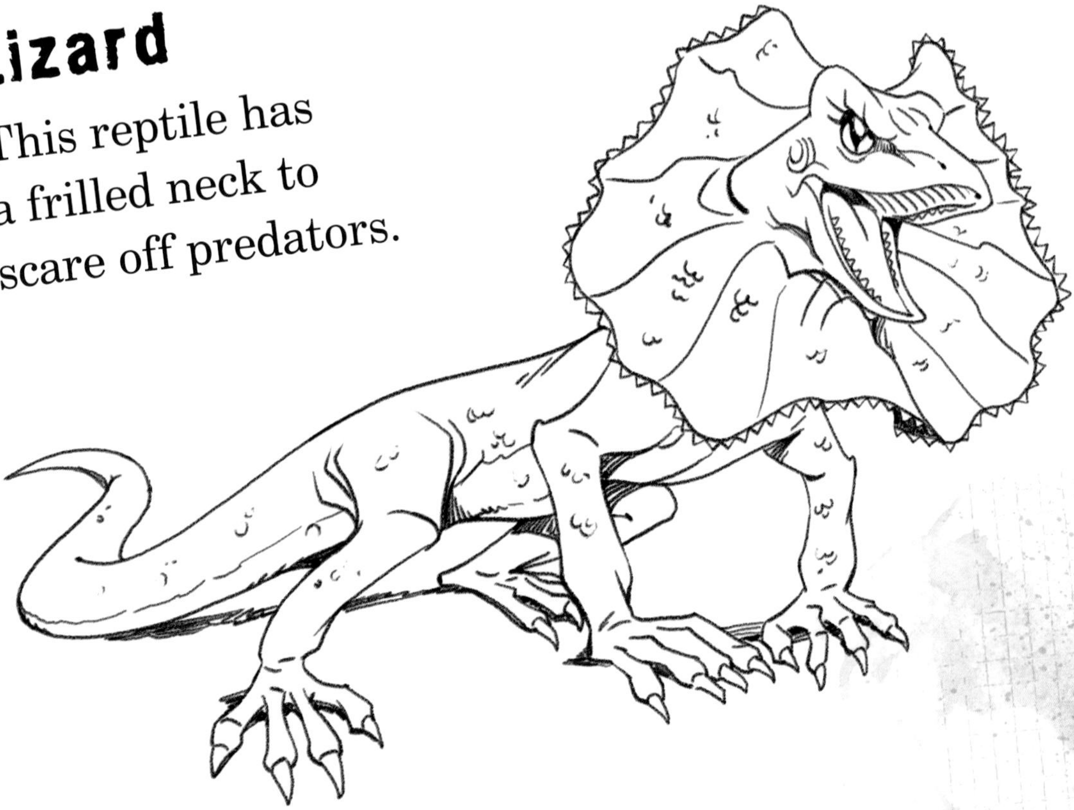

Gorilla

With its large, powerful body, the gorilla is one of the most impressive animals on Earth.

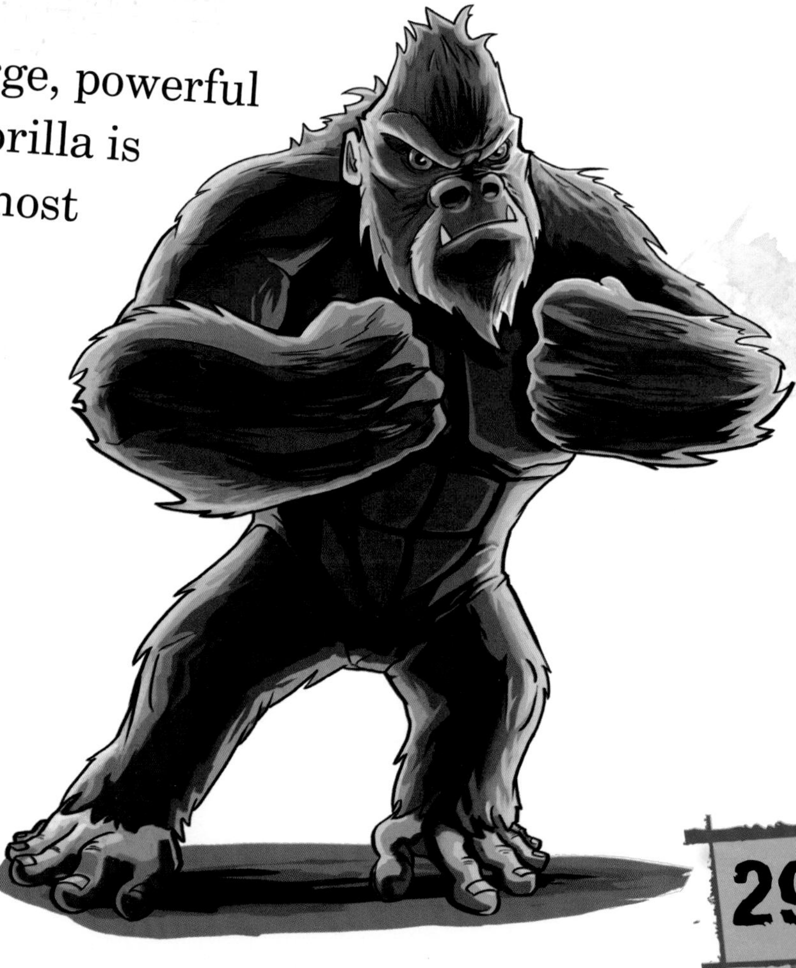

Glossary

agile (A-jul) Able to move with ease.

character (KER-ik-tur) A fictional, or made-up person. Can also mean the features that you recognize something or someone by.

deadly (DED-lee) Can kill.

detail (dih-TAYL) The small, fine lines that are used to add important features to a drawing, such as eyes, horns, and spikes.

erase (ih-RAYS) To remove.

fangs (FANGZ) Sharp teeth.

features (FEE-churz) The eyes, nose, and mouth on a face.

fine-tipped (fyn-TIHPD) A slender, sharp tip to a pencil or pen.

highlights (HY-lytz) Light parts.

injects (in-JEKTS) To make a hole in the skin and pass a liquid into the body.

lunges (LUNJ-ez) Moves suddenly forward.

nostrils (NOS-trulz) The openings on the head or face, through which air is breathed.

predator (PREH-duh-ter) A creature that hunts other creatures for food.

outline (OWT-lyn) A very simple line that provides the shape for a drawing.

palette (PA-lit) A range of colors.

pose (POHZ) The way something or someone stands.

scales (SKALZ) Small, hard shapes that overlap to create a reptile or fish's skin.

shading (SHAYD-ing) Creating lots of lines to add shadow and depth to a drawing.

stallion (STAL-yun) An adult male horse.

venom (VEH-num) An animal's poisonous spit.

Further Reading

Bergin, Mark. *Safari Animals*. It's Fun to Draw. New York: Windmill Books, 2012.

Cook, Trevor, and Lisa Miles. *Drawing Manga*. Drawing Is Fun. New York: Gareth Stevens, 2011.

Hart, Christopher. *Kids Draw Manga Shoujo*. New York: Watson-Guptill, 2005.

Nishida, Masaki. *Drawing Manga Animals*. How to Draw Manga. New York: PowerKids Press, 2008.

Websites

Due to the changing nature of Internet links, PowerKids Press has developed an online list of websites related to the subject of this book. This site is updated regularly. Please use this link to access the list: www.powerkidslinks.com/ltdm/animal/

Index